DECLARATION

•

I hereby declare that
all the paper produced
by Cartiere del Garda S.p.A.
in its Riva del Garda mill
is manufactured completely
Acid-free and Wood-free

Dr. Alois Lueftinger
Managing Director and General Manager
Cartiere del Garda S.p.A.

Earth's Endangered Creatures

SAVE THE TIGER

Written by
Jill Bailey

Illustrated by
Alan Baker

STECK-VAUGHN
LIBRARY
A Division of Steck-Vaughn Company

Austin, Texas

This series is concerned with the world's endangered animals, the reasons why their numbers are diminishing, and the efforts being made to save them from extinction. The author has described these events through the eyes of fictional characters. Although the situations described are based on fact, the people and the events described are fictitious.

**Published in the United States in 1990
by Steck-Vaughn, Co., Austin, Texas,**
a division of National Education Corporation

A Templar Book
Devised and produced by The Templar Company plc
Pippbrook Mill, London Road, Dorking,
Surrey RH4 1JE, Great Britain
Copyright © 1990 by The Templar Company plc
Illustrations copyright © 1990 by The Templar Company plc

Editor Andy Charman
Designer Mike Jolley
Color separations by Positive Colour Ltd,
Maldon, Essex, Great Britain
Printed and bound by L.E.G.O., Vicenza, Italy

1 2 3 4 5 6 7 8 9 0 LE 94 93 92 91 90

Library of Congress Cataloging-in-Publication Data

Bailey, Jill.
Save the Tiger / written by Jill Bailey: illustrated by Alan Baker
p. cm. – (Save our species)
At head of title: Earth's endangered creatures
"A Templar book" – T.p. verso
Summary: Akbar, a tracker for a tourist lodge, works with villagers, would-be poachers, and those involved in Project Tiger to protect the diminishing number of tigers in his part of India.
ISBN 0-8114-2703-X
[1. Tigers–Fiction. 2. Wildlife conservation–Fiction. 3. India–Fiction]
I. Baker, Alan., ill.   II. Title.
III. Title: Earth's endangered creatures.
IV. Series.
PZ7.B1525Sav   1990   89-48770
[Fic] – dc20   CIP AC

CONTENTS

TRACKING THE TIGER
page 6

HUNTING THE TIGER
page 18

PROJECT TIGER
page 28

TIGER UPDATE
page 44

INDEX
page 46

TRACKING THE TIGER

Akbar Singh watched the curls of wood smoke rising from the village below him. All around him lay fields and terraces of neat plots planted with corn, beans, and fruit trees. A mile away lay the forest, now part of the tiger reserve.

On a small hill near the edge of the village sat Akbar's creeper-draped wooden house. His father, a forester, had built it in the days before the village existed. In those days, tigers and leopards would pass by in the night, leaving their tracks in the mud by the water pump. Then the settlers had come, clearing trees and planting crops. As their natural home shrank, the tigers started coming into the village.

Last week a man had been attacked as he worked in a sugar-cane field. A few days later a buffalo was taken from right outside a house. The people were frightened. It was part of Akbar's job as a tracker for the tourist lodge to investigate. He walked down to the scene of the attack. The sugarcane was nearly ripe and taller than a man.

Eventually, Akbar found the tiger's tracks. They were large footprints, the tracks of an adult male, probably old "Long Claws." One imprint was deeper than the other, and strangely distorted. The tiger must have been limping. Could this be the reason why he could not catch and kill his usual prey? Akbar decided to find out by setting a trap. The team from Project Tiger would be able to knock out the animal with a tranquilizing dart. Then he would be able to look at the injured foot.

Years ago there were few houses and the forest was home to many tigers. Now tigers are very scarce.

The rules of the tiger reserve forbid the farmers to plant tall crops close to the forest. They are good cover for a prowling tiger.

The valley was thick with mist as Andy Rowland and Akbar Singh set out with the elephants. They were a mixed crowd – the three huge animals, the elephant keepers in their turbans, the rangers in uniform, and Andy in jeans and T-shirt. Akbar and the rangers were armed with dart guns to tranquilize the tiger.

Andy had been in India for six weeks and was now a regular visitor on the rangers' excursions. He was

The rangers were armed with dart guns. They would not be used to kill the tiger, but to put it to sleep.

trying to record the number of tigers in the reserve, their age, sex, size, and health. This information would show the rangers how their work was helping to save the tiger. If they could capture this animal, he could measure it and check its teeth. He would also make a sketch of the patterns on its skin. Each tiger has different markings. With the sketch, Andy could recognize this tiger if he saw it again.

Slowly the party made its way past the sugarcane and into the forest. Soon they had picked up the strange tracks of the injured animal. They were close to the spot where Akbar had tethered a deer. One of the rangers signaled them to halt. The tiger was in sight. Andy raised his binoculars. The old male tiger was crouched on the ground, feeding on the deer's carcass. Akbar aimed his dart gun, and fired.

The tiger started, got up hastily and then swayed. It staggered a few steps across the clearing, then sank to the ground. Akbar and Andy climbed down and crept up to the drugged tiger. It was all right – the tiger was asleep and snoring gently. Akbar examined its feet. Sure enough, a bad wound on one of its front paws was pushing the toes apart.

The elephants watched everything quietly. They were not afraid. Tigers rarely attack large animals.

Andy held the huge golden paw firmly as Akbar cleaned the wound with antiseptic. A large thorn could be seen stuck between the tiger's toes. Akbar pulled at the thorn. It wouldn't move. He fetched some pliers from his bag and tried again. This time it moved – all 4 inches of it. It was not a thorn, but a porcupine quill.

"I'm surprised that they try to tackle porcupines," commented Andy. "How can a tiger kill such a dangerous animal?"

"The tiger has to be quick and grab the porcupine from in front before it can jab in its quills and run away. The quills come off and are left in the tiger's face or paws. The wounds often get infected." Akbar gently injected an antibiotic into the wound.

Before the tiger woke up, they measured it. It was an old male, 10 feet long and 3 feet at the shoulder.

"Not the biggest I've seen," said Akbar. "They can reach a length of 11 feet and weigh over 650 pounds. The females are smaller 9 feet long at most."

Andy examined the tiger's teeth. The huge pointed canines were in good condition for an old tiger. It was still quite able to kill and hold its prey. He made a quick sketch of the pattern on the tiger's head. Then they all climbed back onto the elephants and waited to make sure that the animal recovered properly from the tranquilizer.

The tiger's eyelids fluttered. His paws twitched. Then he opened his eyes fully and gazed blearily at the watchers. He struggled to lift himself, but fell back on the ground with a surprised look on his face. After several attempts, he struggled shakily to his feet and walked unsteadily into the undergrowth.

The tiger slept soundly for 30 minutes. In that time, Akbar was able to clean the wounded paw.

The canines, used to pierce and grip prey, are the sharp, pointed teeth on either side of the front teeth.

The party turned back toward the village.

"Aren't you afraid he will attack someone again?" asked Andy. "After all, his paw is still very sore." Akbar told him not to worry.

"We shall leave food out for him until his paw has healed. He is only dangerous because he is hungry. We can build a *machan* – a tree hideout – near the food, so we can keep an eye on him."

Andy was curious.

"Are all man-eating tigers hurt?"

"No," said Akbar. "Some old tigers have lost their teeth, so they can't kill their prey. Sometimes there isn't any prey to catch. When the villagers shoot deer or pigs that wander into their fields, the tiger runs out of his usual prey, and starts taking cattle. That takes him nearer to the village, so he is more likely to meet humans.

"Tigers don't naturally have a taste for humans," continued Akbar, "but it can happen accidentally. A tigress may attack and kill a man who happens to come between her and her cubs. She's only trying to defend her cubs – it's the natural thing for her to do. Then she eats part of the body and gets used to the taste.

"Tigers only seem to recognize humans who are standing up. If a person is bending down, the tiger may mistake him or her for another animal and attack."

Andy was not convinced.

"There seem to be a lot of man-eater stories around," he said.

"Don't believe all you hear," warned Akbar. "Man-eater claims make good cover-ups for murder. A man will kill someone, drag the body into the forest, and claim that he was killed by a tiger.

The villagers still went into the forest even though they had been warned not to. Attacks by tigers were increasing in number.

"The villagers, who are frightened of tigers anyway, are always ready to believe such stories, and an innocent tiger has to be shot."

The cubs stay with their mother for two years. She will protect them against anything, even male tigers that are stronger than herself.

Tigers also live in tropical rain forests in other parts of India.

Saving the tiger means saving these forests as well.

As the party crossed the river, they were met by a crowd of villagers. They were excited, and shouted to Akbar.

"Did you kill the tiger?"

"Are we safe now?"

Akbar explained how he had treated the wounded tiger. The villagers were unhappy.

"None of us will be safe after dark," said one of them.

"If you won't take care of him," said another, "we'll have to shoot him ourselves."

Akbar reminded them that killing tigers was illegal.

"And so is planting sugarcane next to the reserve," he added. Prithviraj, one of the village elders, moved forward to argue.

"We need the cane, we can't graze our cattle in the forest, so how else can we make a living?"

"You can plant the cane on the other side of the village," said Akbar. "It will be safer there. You are given free firewood and thatch. If you graze in the forest and destroy it, where will the firewood come from then?"

Prithviraj wasn't impressed.

"Why can't we use the forest the way our fathers and grandfathers did? There were plenty of tigers in the early days."

"So there were," retorted Akbar, "but there were only 20 to 30 villagers then. Now there are four times as many people and far fewer tigers. Also, you have medicines, more and more children survive, and one day they too will graze cattle. The whole forest will not be big enough for them. Why don't you take up the Project Tiger offer of a new village in the Chambal Valley? The soil is good. You could have a school, a clinic, and a place to meet. There's even land to plant trees for firewood, so it won't need to come from the forest."

Some of the villagers could see that the move made sense. They started arguing with each other. Akbar and Andy slipped away.

Akbar spoke to Prithviraj about moving to the Chambal Valley. The people could live there without damaging the forest.

The afternoon sun was bathing the village in a shimmering, hazy heat as Akbar set out to check on the old tiger. He had left a carcass out the night before, and wanted to see if the injured animal had eaten it. He crossed the bridge and followed a small path above the river. Suddenly he heard the sound of splashing a little farther ahead. Akbar crept forward as quietly as he could, wishing the leaves beneath his feet were not so dry and crackly.

A tigress was sitting in the cool water almost up to her neck. She was watching her cubs make their first attempts to swim. Tigers like to spend the hot afternoons in the water, out of reach of flies.

Akbar climbed the hill and turned into the patch of thorn scrub where he had left the carcass. The vultures had found it – he could hear them squabbling. As he approached, they flew off noisily. There was not much meat left, but the lame tiger's tracks showed that he had been here, probably during the night.

Akbar returned the way he had come. The cubs were now playing happily in the shallow water. Suddenly, the tigress coughed. The cubs leaped out of the water and disappeared into the bushes. She began to snarl, and Akbar saw a large male tiger, one he had not seen before. The tigress backed away, still snarling. Akbar knew that the old, lame tiger would soon move away, for he would not want to share a territory with a younger and stronger rival.

Of all the big cats, tigers are the most at home in the water. They swim well, but dislike getting their faces wet. They enter the water slowly, walking backward, keeping a watchful eye on the bank.

HUNTING THE TIGER

Vinod led the old water buffalo quietly along the path. He listened for any rustle in the bushes that might signal a tiger's approach. Soon he found the tracks of a grown tigress and a cub's smaller marks leading into the undergrowth.

He moved on toward his hideout. It was on the edge of a clearing, set among the branches at a safe height above the ground. Tethering the buffalo to a tree as bait, he climbed up, loaded his rifle, and settled down to wait. It was almost dark. If only she would come tonight. A skin as beautiful as hers would feed his family until the next monsoon. It might even pay for his son to return to school.

There was a sound below him. Vinod tensed, then exclaimed angrily as he recognized his cousin, Akbar. Akbar was an expert tracker. He worked for the tourist lodge. One of his jobs was to lead tourists to the tigers in the reserve. These days they wanted to photograph the animals, not shoot them. The visitors brought much needed money into the area, but the tigers caused many problems. They were doing well in the reserve. Now they were wandering into the surrounding villages, taking livestock, and endangering the villagers' lives.

Why had Akbar come? Was he going to turn Vinod in to the authorities for poaching? The light was fading fast. Akbar's presence might well keep the tigress away. If she approached, however, Akbar would be in great danger, for he was now standing between the tigress's lair and the bait. Gripping his rifle firmly, Vinod strained to see in the shadows.

The water buffalo grazed lazily. It was unaware of any danger.

The village was close to the reserve. The tigers were coming out of the forest and taking livestock.

Akbar climbed up to his cousin.

"I thought I'd find you here – Nalini told me she saw you crossing the bridge with the animal."

Vinod scolded him.

"What are you doing here?"

"I came to ask you not to shoot this one," said Akbar. "You realize she has a cub?"

"Of course," replied Vinod, "I saw the tracks, but there are too many tigers around. What does it matter?"

"Killing tigers is punishable with prison," warned Akbar.

"You wouldn't report me – the family would never speak to you again. How will your son Sanjay get a job if his uncles don't put in a good word for him?"

"Vinod," argued Akbar, "if you kill the females with cubs, where is the next generation of tigers going to come from? There will be nothing for you to shoot."

"There are plenty more tigers in the reserve," said Vinod. "There are more tigers than the reserve can feed. That's why they are killing people's cattle."

"No, it isn't," said Akbar. "It's because the villagers have shot all the deer and the tigers have nothing left to eat. You kill the deer because they eat your grass, then the tigers kill your cattle – you have gained nothing!"

The tigress crept carefully out of the undergrowth. She could hear the buffalo as it moved in the grass.

"Exactly!" argued Vinod. "If there were no tigers, the cattle would be safe, and tourists wouldn't come nosing around our villages."

"That's true," Akbar said quietly. "And if there were no tigers, there would be no forest. We would lose all the wildlife that lives there. The tourists wouldn't come and many people would lose their jobs. The trees would be cut down to make room for crops. You know that the crops wouldn't be your own. You would have to work on someone else's farm. The women would have to walk for miles each day to find firewood."

Vinod scowled at his cousin. There was a rustle below them. The tigress had come for the buffalo. Perhaps she had heard the two men, for she turned her head toward them, her eyes blazing in the light from the fading sunset.

Vinod and Akbar froze. It seemed that the tigress was staring straight at them.

The tigress placed one paw on the tree, raised her head, and sniffed the air. For a moment, the two men feared she had detected them.

Then, after what seemed like an hour, she looked away. The buffalo sensed danger and became nervous. The tigress kept her distance from it, moving around until she was almost behind it. Then she waited. The buffalo relaxed, and began grazing again. Suddenly the tigress struck, leaping toward the buffalo and swiping at one of its back legs with her front paw. The leg buckled. As the buffalo fell, the tigress was on its back, her teeth sinking into its throat. It was all over in a minute. Like a true tiger, she had made a clean kill. Death followed so swiftly that the buffalo felt almost no pain.

The tigress began to feed while the men watched. Vinod was dismayed to see the tigress's fur rapidly becoming matted and bloody. The tigress looked up from her kill and moaned softly. The cub emerged from the bushes. He would now eat. Vinod slowly raised his gun and took aim. Furiously, Akbar knocked it out of his grasp. The tree shook and the gun fell to the ground.

In a moment the tigress was on her feet, roaring with anger. She leaped at the tree, pounding it with her paws.

"I hope the *machan* is sturdy enough," whispered Akbar.

"Well, you've made sure we have no gun to defend ourselves with," snapped Vinod.

The tigress snarled up at them, her eyes blazing. Then she moved back a few feet and sat down in the long, dry grass, keeping her eyes firmly fixed on the branches of the tree. What could they do now?

Tigers eat every scrap of meat on an animal kill. The tiger on the right is feeding. He growls as a warning to the intruder not to come closer.

The cub followed his mother into the clearing. He was about 8 months old and growing fast. His mother had to kill every two days in order to feed him.

It was getting light as Andy and Sunil approached the machan. *The elephant gently lifted the stranded men onto its back.*

The clock struck midnight. Andy Rowland glanced up from his desk. Akbar had been gone too long. He had a feeling that something was wrong. Grabbing his flashlight, he went across to talk to Sunil, one of the reserve guards. It was Sunil's job to protect the tigers from poachers.

"Do you have any idea where he was going?" asked Andy. "He left five hours ago, and he promised to call in on the way home."

"Let's see if we can find his tracks," suggested Sunil, obviously worried. The ground was dry and dusty, and they soon picked up Akbar's footprints. As they entered the forest, Sunil stopped.

"Look," he said. "There are two sets of tracks – someone was here before Akbar."

They heard a low rumbling sound close by.

"Tiger!" exclaimed Sunil. The men crept forward until they could see the tigress. She was still watching the *machan*.

"That must be the tigress with the cub," said Sunil. "She's much too dangerous to approach. We should get an elephant."

They walked quietly back to the sleeping village and untethered a large elephant. As they approached the machan again, the tigress snarled and backed away. She growled with irritation.

"Who's there?" Akbar's anxious voice called out from the *machan*.

"Andy and Sunil," cried Andy. "We've brought an elephant."

Akbar and Vinod clambered out onto a branch and the elephant gently lifted each man onto its back. Turning to Vinod, Andy asked, "Did you come out to watch the tiger?"

"Er … yes … er … we had a good view from the machan," replied Vinod. He made a mental note to return later to fetch his gun before Akbar could take it away.

It is against the law to shoot tigers for their skins. Vinod's family was poor. He could earn more money hunting than he could farming.

The sale of products made from the tiger is also illegal. Tiger-skin coats are still sold for huge amounts of money. Traders like Terhua get very rich.

Terhua was waiting for Vinod. Terhua was not his real name – but no one here knew that. The name meant "crooked," a good name for a dealer in illegal skins. Vinod opened the door. He was scared of Terhua.

"So you haven't got a skin for me," said Terhua, angrily.

Vinod explained that he had dropped his gun while climbing a tree to avoid a tigress.

"I'll try again tomorrow," offered Vinod, "but one of the guards is suspicious. It might be better if I took a leopard instead."

"A leopard isn't as valuable as a tiger skin," said Terhua, "and you owe me for the new gun I bought you. I want a decent tiger skin – without messy bullet holes."

"But how do I kill a tiger without bullets?" asked Vinod, puzzled.

"Poison," said Terhua, simply. "Get hold of some insecticide the villagers spray on their crops, and poison a carcass with it."

They were interrupted by Vinod's wife, Nalini. Terhua did not look at her, said goodbye, and left.

"I don't like that man," said Nalini. "Why work for him?"

"How else will I make good money?" asked Vinod.

"We don't need so much money," said Nalini.

"But I have to pay for the new gun," protested Vinod.

"If you weren't poaching, you wouldn't need the gun," retorted Nalini. "You're a good tracker and you know the forest – why don't you train as a forester?"

"I would have to go to Delhi to train," replied Vinod. "Anyway, Terhua wouldn't like it – things could get nasty." He scowled. "I'm going to get my gun."

"Your new gun? Where is it?" asked Nalini.

"In the forest," said Vinod, and slammed out of the house.

If Vinod couldn't kill a tiger, he would have to get a leopard. It was not worth as much, but he could still go to prison for shooting it.

PROJECT TIGER

Andy Rowland looked back at the sleeping village from the cart he was riding on. It was hard to believe he had been here only six weeks. Already the forest had become part of his life. At night he lay awake listening to its sounds. At dawn he liked to be outside studying tracks.

The ox cart rattled down the rough road toward the railroad station. The train would get him to Delhi in time to meet his girlfriend, Sara. She would be on the plane from London.

The plane was late, so Andy made his way to the zoo. Delhi Zoo was a delightful place – not a concrete jungle of cages and bars. There were 100 acres of green

About 60 people lived in the village. Their houses were built of wood from the forest.

Brijendra had been a keeper at the zoo for 15 years. His knowledge of how tigers behave in the zoo would help to save them in the wild.

park with large enclosures shaded by trees and bushes.

The tigers were cooling off lazily in the lagoon, to the delight of the tourists. Andy went to find their keeper, Brijendra Bedi.

"We are proud of our Indian tigers," Brijendra boasted. "Savitri, the tigress you see in the lagoon, produced four fine cubs last year."

"Four seems a lot – do tigers usually have so many cubs?" asked Andy.

"They can have up to six cubs," replied Brijendra.

"I think seven is the record, but that's very rare. Usually they have two or three. The tigress will not breed again until the cubs have left home, which may be 18 months later. That's one reason why tiger populations take so long to recover from over-hunting."

"What happens if the cubs die young?" asked Andy.

"The tigress will come into heat –that is, be ready to breed again – sooner." A loud roar interrupted their conversation. Andy and Brijendra rushed to the tiger compound.

In zoos it is possible to study closely how tigers breed. This information will be useful to anyone trying to save tigers in the wild.

Savitri, the tigress, roared again, and glared at a man who was throwing bread at her.

"They do it to make her roar," sighed Brijendra.

"What happens to the cubs when they grow up?" asked Andy.

"We sell them to other zoos, or we keep them to replace tigers that are too old to breed."

"Couldn't you release them into the wild?" Andy suggested.

"Unfortunately not," replied

The tiger's hunting skills can only be learned in the wild. Stalking a sambar requires patience and cunning.

Brijendra. "To survive in the wild a tiger needs many skills which take over a year to learn, and can only be taught by its mother. That's why cubs spend so long with their mothers. Many of our tigresses were born in a zoo, so they have no jungle experience to pass on."

Andy was curious. "So is it really useful to breed them in zoos?".

"A few years ago zoos were the only hope of saving the tiger. The Chinese tiger hasn't been seen in the wild for many years, but there are about 40 surviving in zoos. The Indian tiger was going the same way before Project Tiger was started. In zoos we have the chance to study some of the tiger's behavior – mating and birth, for instance. This may help us to understand better how to protect them in the wild."

"What about people who visit the zoo?" asked Andy.

"Zoos make them aware of how beautiful these animals are. Once you've seen them so close, it's hard to imagine killing them. However, now that there's TV, people don't need to come to zoos to see tigers."

Andy thought of the wildlife films that had first fired his interest in tigers. They captured the sights and sounds of tiger country in a way zoos never could. Still, there was something exciting about seeing the living animal so close, looking into those amber eyes.

White tigers are found in many zoos. They are all descended from a white tiger cub that was once kept as a pet by the Maharajah of Rewa.

Andy and Sara entered the dark shop which smelled of leather, glue, and Indian spices. They had decided to investigate reports that the owner was trading in illegal skins.

"We'll say we want to buy a leopard-skin rug," Andy whispered.

The shopkeeper was sitting in a corner, braiding a leather belt. When Andy made his request, the man looked at him sharply.

"We have no illegal skins here," he said.

"We're not the law," said Andy. "A friend in Khandela said you can get skins if we place a firm order."

"Ah!" The shopkeeper thought for a while. "You want to see my house? Mohan!" A clerk appeared from a back room. "Look after the shop – I'm going out for a while."

Andy and Sara followed him out to his rickety old car. They drove through the winding streets to the outskirts of the city, and pulled up outside a large, white house surrounded by trees. Obviously the skin trade paid well! The basement was lined with skins – leopard, jungle cat, lizard, snake – and tiger. The trader spread out a small leopard-skin rug on the floor.

"How many of these skins do you sell?" asked Andy.

"It depends," the man replied. "I sell perhaps 2,000 small skins a year and about 10 tiger skins."

"Can we get the skins out of India?"

"Of course, it's not legal – but there are ways – on foot over the hills to Pakistan, or perhaps in a small plane. It is risky and expensive! It's better to keep them in this country and say that they are old skins."

The skin-dealer's shop was just a ramshackle hut in a market square. Nobody would have guessed by looking at it how much money this man made.

A tiger-skin rug may sell for thousands of dollars, but Vinod was paid only $200 for the skin.

"How much is this one?" asked Sara, stroking the leopard skin.

"Fifteen hundred dollars. I can get bigger ones."

"I'll have to think it over," stalled Sara. "Can we call you?"

The trader frowned. "You don't want to buy? You want only to look! OK, you can call me, but now you'll have to go."

The next day Andy took Sara into the reserve. Sambar deer were standing in the lake grazing on waterweeds. A small group of chital, or axis deer, stood drinking on the bank. Beyond the lake were more hills, and an occasional ruined fortress half-hidden in the trees.

"There used to be a village over there," remarked Andy, "but

Chital spend most of their time grazing peacefully near lakes.

Project Tiger paid for a new village outside the reserve, and the people moved. Now we don't allow people into this part of the reserve, so the tigers are not disturbed. Around the edge of the forest we let people hunt a limited number of animals – except tigers, of course! We have to fence out their cattle, but we allow villagers into the reserve at certain times of the year. They gather fodder for their animals, straw for thatching, fruit, and wild honey."

"What kind of animals are in the water?" asked Sara.

"They're sambar deer, the tiger's main prey. The smaller ones on the bank are chital. Tigers eat them, too." Sara was fascinated; this was all so new to her.

"What else do tigers eat?" she asked.

"Wild pigs, peacocks, langur monkeys – when they are on the ground – and buffalo."

Sara pointed to a loglike object slowly moving toward the sambar.

"Is that a crocodile?"

"Yes!" replied Andy. "Crocodiles sometimes kill sambar, but their teeth aren't strong enough to break open the skins. They have to wait for the carcass to rot. Often the tigers steal the carcass."

There was a loud commotion in the lake as the crocodile attacked. The sambar leapt through the water. This time, the crocodile had struck without success.

Sambar deer wade into the lake to feed on waterweeds. They might be attacked at any moment by crocodiles, which patrol the water looking for an easy meal.

The young male tiger could be seen prowling around the lake in the mornings and late afternoons. He was marking his new territory.

A chital sounded a high-pitched alarm. A figure appeared in the distance, and was making its way around the lake toward them. It was Akbar, on his way home.

"How many tigers are there here?" Sara asked.

"About 25 in the whole reserve," replied Andy. "At the moment there are two males, two females, and a cub in the area around the lake. Now that a young male has arrived, the old one will soon move away. He is too old to fight and will lose his territory."

"What do you mean – territory?" queried Sara.

"An area the tiger regards as its own. A tiger does not like another tiger to live too close. For one thing, there might not be enough food to go around. For another, he wants exclusive rights to the local tigresses."

"But how does a tiger know he is in another tiger's territory?"

"He uses scent," said Andy. "A tiger sprays urine on bushes and trees as he walks around his territory. The urine contains a special chemical that gives it a distinctive smell. Each tiger's smell is different, telling whether the resident animal is male or female, and how recently it passed that way. Tigresses have a special smell when

Tigers have territories of 6 to 18 square miles. Lakes are important to these territories, because of the animals that feed there.

they are in heat – this tells the male tigers that they are ready to mate."

"Have you ever seen tigers mating?" asked Sara.

"No. Very few people have, except in zoos. Akbar has. Here he is now. You can ask him about it."

Akbar sat on the ground beside Andy and Sara.

"Mating is a very affectionate affair," he explained. "At first, the tigress snarls when the male approaches. She has to make sure he is not threatening her. The male may lie down to show he is not going to attack. Once the tigress is sure of him, she will rub herself against his side, and nuzzle up to him. The couple will walk around each other, sniffing, licking, and nibbling gently at each other.

"When the tiger is ready to mate, he comes up behind the female and grips her by the neck, with his teeth. After mating, the female usually snarls at him and backs away. Then she lies on her back and rests. Tigers may mate many times over several days."

In the morning, Sara joined Andy on his daily rounds of the reserve.

They stopped beside some tracks in the road.

"Tigers like to use the road; it is clear and they can move more quietly," Andy explained. He placed a piece of glass over the track, covered it with tracing paper, and drew the outline of the footprint.

"Sometimes we also make plaster casts of the tracks. This one is a male, you can tell from the size. The male's pads can be twice the size of the female's. Akbar would be able to tell you exactly which tiger this is. He knows by the shape of the toes and the depth of the track. A large, heavy tiger makes a deeper print. Let's look for some other signs."

Courtship and mating can take place at any time of the year. Few people have seen this happen in the wild.

The best way to identify a tiger is by its pugmarks – footprints. An adult male's pugmarks can be twice the size of the female's.

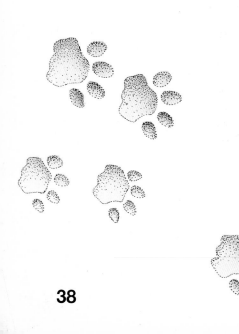

"Why do you have to record all the tracks?" asked Sara.

"So we can tell how many tigers there are in the reserve, and what their movements are," replied Andy. "It helps us learn about their behavior, how much space they need, and so on."

"Is that what Project Tiger is all about?"

"Oh, it's much, much more than that. I've invited Akbar to supper tonight. He'll tell you all about it. Let's look for some more signs."

Andy pointed to the trunk of a tree leaning over the path. "See those scratch marks? They're tiger claw marks. Big tigers claw the bark higher up than smaller tigers."

"There's a strong smell," remarked Sara.

"That's not the scratches," said Andy, and he pointed to the side of the track. "There's some tiger dung, and some more scratch marks. Another way of marking territory. The smell is very strong. These

---

Tigers mark their territories by scratching trees. Other tigers keep well away. They rarely fight among themselves.

must be fresh droppings – the tiger isn't far away."

Sara felt a sinking feeling in her stomach.

"Do you think it can smell us?" she asked.

"I'm sure it already has," replied Andy, "but tigers aren't interested in humans, except to keep out of their way. If it were a female with cubs, we would be in danger – a tigress will attack any creature that comes near her cubs."

Sara was puzzled. "You mean to say her mate doesn't defend them?" she asked.

"The tiger leaves the tigress as soon as they have mated. The tigress gives birth to her cubs after 15 weeks. They are born blind and helpless. For this reason, she keeps them in a den. This will be close to a source of food. It is a very secret place, so secret that it's impossible to find. Even Akbar, who's an expert, has never seen cubs younger than three months."

The male tiger leaves the female as soon as they have mated. He then returns to his own territory or moves on to find another female.

As they sipped hot tea in the flickering candlelight after supper, Akbar explained how Project Tiger was born.

"In 1930 there were about 100,000 tigers in Asia. Sadly, hunters were still shooting tigers as trophies, and the tigers' natural home, the forest, was being gradually destroyed. By 1940, only about 40,000 tigers were left in India, and by 1969 the tiger was in danger of disappearing altogether. Only 1,800 were left.

"In 1972 Operation Tiger was born. It later became known as Project Tiger. The World Wide Fund for Nature (WWF) offered the Indian government money to

This boat from Sunderbans mangrove swamps has been electrified by a Project Tiger team. The tiger receives a mild shock, and will, perhaps, not attack again.

Local people work for Project Tiger as antipoaching guards.

help create a series of special tiger reserves. Mrs. Gandhi, the Indian Prime Minister, set up a Tiger Task Force the very next day, and other countries, such as Bangladesh and Nepal, soon joined the program. An international treaty was signed by many countries. It banned trade in endangered animals, and this has also helped to save the tiger."

"Is it expensive to set up reserves?" asked Sara.

"Creating reserves isn't easy," replied Akbar. "We have to consider the local people. There isn't always enough land for cattle and wild deer to graze. The tigers eat the deer, so it's important that there are enough of them in the reserve. Tourists bring money into the area. We employ many local people. They control forest and grass fires, and work as guards to prevent poaching. For this we need roads and guard huts, guns, binoculars, two-way radios, water, and other supplies. It all costs a lot of money."

"Do you have enough reserves now?" asked Sara. Akbar smiled.

"We can never have enough," he said, "but I think we have saved the tiger. There are over 4,000 tigers in India today, and the population is increasing. It's not only the tigers that have been saved. It's the whole forest. Inside the reserves, deer, antelope, rare birds, butterflies, and plants have also multiplied. Our grandchildren will inherit the forest just as we inherited it, with all its dangers and beauties and valuable resources.

"Project Tiger has been very successful. So many people from all over the world have raised money for us, with charity walks and other fund-raising events. The tiger has many friends."

There are now 15 Project Tiger reserves in India. They are set up in the best tiger areas.

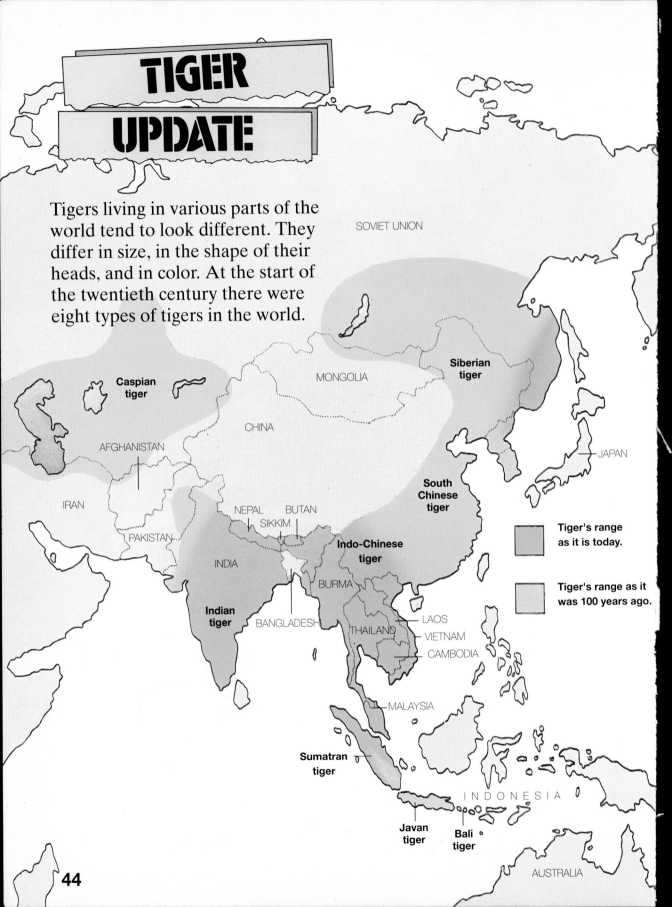

TIGER UPDATE

Tigers living in various parts of the world tend to look different. They differ in size, in the shape of their heads, and in color. At the start of the twentieth century there were eight types of tigers in the world.

SOVIET UNION

Caspian tiger

MONGOLIA

Siberian tiger

CHINA

AFGHANISTAN

JAPAN

IRAN

NEPAL   BUTAN

SIKKIM

South Chinese tiger

PAKISTAN

Indo-Chinese tiger

INDIA

BURMA

Indian tiger

BANGLADESH

LAOS

THAILAND

VIETNAM

CAMBODIA

Tiger's range as it is today.

Tiger's range as it was 100 years ago.

MALAYSIA

Sumatran tiger

INDONESIA

Javan tiger

Bali tiger

AUSTRALIA

44

The Siberian Tiger • This is the largest of the tigers. It lives in far eastern Russia and part of northeastern China. There are about 300 surviving in the wild, but over 600 in zoos.

The Caspian Tiger • A medium-sized tiger with closely striped fur, it once ranged from the Caspian Sea to Iran, Afghanistan, and the Soviet Union. It is thought to be extinct.

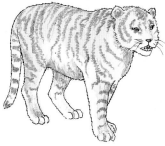

The Indian Tiger • This race has the largest population today, about 4,000. A medium-sized tiger with a short glossy coat of rich golden brown, it lives in a variety of habitats.

The Chinese or Manchurian Tiger • The Chinese tiger is now feared to be extinct in the wild – none has been seen for many years, but about 40 survive in zoos around the world.

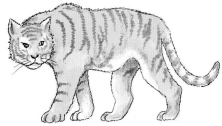

The Javan Tiger • From the island of Java, the Javan tiger is almost certainly extinct. It was the smallest race, with a rather dark coat.

The Bali Tiger • The Bali tiger was already rare in 1900, and the last one was shot in 1937.

The Indo-Chinese Tiger • The Indo-Chinese tiger is found from southern China and eastern Burma to Vietnam and Malaysia. There are probably fewer than 50 in the wild.

The Sumatran Tiger • From the island of Sumatra, this tiger is threatened due to uncontrolled poaching and the loss of the forest. About 150 Sumatran tigers are in zoos.

INDEX

A
antipoaching patrol 42

B
Bali tiger 45
birth 31, 41
breeding 29, 31

C
Caspian tiger 45
cattle 12, 15, 20-21, 35, 43
Chinese tiger 31, 45
chital 34, 35, 36
courtship 38
crops 8, 21, 26
cubs 12-13, 16, 18, 20, 22, 25, 29, 30, 36, 41

D
darting gun 8-9
deer 9, 12, 20, 34-35, 43
Delhi 27, 28-29
dung 40

E
elephants 8-9, 10, 24, 25

F
firewood 15, 21
fodder 35
footprints 38
forest 6, 9, 12, 14, 15, 21, 24, 27, 28, 35, 42

G
Ghandi, Mrs. 43
guards 24, 27, 42

H
hunting skills 10, 30

I
Indian tiger 31, 45
Indo-Chinese tiger 45

J
Javan tiger 45

L
langur monkeys 35
leopard 27
leopard-skin rug 32-33
livestock 18, 19

M
machan 12, 22, 24, 25
man-eating tigers 12, 15
markings 8-9, 10
mating 31, 37-38

P
poachers 18, 24, 27, 43
poison 27
prey 10, 11, 12, 35
Project Tiger 6, 15, 31, 40, 42-43
pugmarks 38

R
rangers 8-9
reserve 6, 7, 15, 18, 19, 20, 34-36, 38, 40, 42-43

S
scent 37
Siberian tiger 45

size 8, 10
skin trade 32-33
skins 26-27, 32-33
sugarcane 6, 9, 15
Sumatran tiger 45

T
teeth 8, 10, 11, 12
territory 16, 36-37, 40-41
tiger-skin rugs 32-33
Tiger Task Force 43
tigress 12, 16, 18, 20, 21-22, 25, 27, 29, 30, 36-37, 38, 41
tourist lodge 6, 18
tourists 18, 21, 29, 43
trackers 6, 18, 27
tracks 6, 9, 18, 20, 24-25, 28, 38, 40
tranquilizing dart 6, 8-9, 10

V
villages 6, 12, 15, 16, 18, 19, 21, 25, 28

W
water 16-17, 29, 34-35
water buffalo 18, 21, 22, 35
weight 10
white tigers 31
wildlife 21
World Wide Fund for Nature 42
wounds 9-10, 15

Z
zoo 28-29, 30-31